This book belongs to.

_____

_____

_____

_____

THE ADVENTURES OF

LiLY-MAY

FOUL FAERIES

WRITTEN BY EMMA-JANE LEESON
ILLUSTRATED BY SALLY-ANN KELLY

First published 2021 by The Johnny Magory Co. Ltd.

This edition published 2022 by The Johnny Magory Co. Ltd.

Ballynafagh, Prosperous, Naas, Co. Kildare, Ireland

Text, illustrations and design © Emma-Jane Leeson

ISBN: 978-1-8382152-9-3

We're an independent Irish business who believe in keeping it local in all that we do. Here's how and where this little book was made:

Written & Designed by Emma-Jane Leeson, Co. Kildare

Illustrated by Sally-Ann Kelly, Co. Kildare

Printed by Anglo Printers, Co. Louth

We also believe in helping our planet. This book has been produced with sustainably sourced paper and free from plastic.

There's no need to continue reading this boring bit unless you're planning on getting up to no good (at which point we'd really love to hear from you to see if we can get in on the act too!)

I would like to split this dedication in two…

Firstly, this is for Moggy, for enduring my awful stories as a teenager and for being polite enough to not demand I stop writing them for you.

Secondly, this is for the children who continue to grow up and be magnificent. Thank you for enjoying my earlier books and for giving me the nudge to take more stories from my head and put them on paper.

EJ

Let me tell you a story

About Johnny Magory

His sister Lily-May

And their trusty dog Ruairi...

Chapter 1

Into the Magical Wild

"It's very early for you to be going exploring Johnny, just be careful and make sure you're back in time for lunch, ok? Love you," Mammy said as her son put his empty porridge bowl in the sink and raced out by her.

"Yeah, yeah, yeah! Love you too Ma," Johnny said as he leapt out the back door and slammed it behind him.

She's obsessed with me having lunch, he thought to himself as he ran across the garden towards the rabbit hole tunnel. It was the twenty-first of June, the summer solstice, and the early morning sun shone bright and warm on Ireland. Johnny was bursting with excitement for this long-awaited day to finally arrive. The longest day of the year meant the longest party of the year… But this was going to be a party he'd never forget.

As he was crouching down to enter into the rabbit hole that was at the bottom of the hedge around his garden, a fluffy brown head with two deep brown eyes appeared in front of him. Before he could move back, he felt it lick his face.

"Ruairi!" Johnny cried, "I've told you before boy, I'm too old for kisses!"

Ruairi lowered his head with a little whimper, Ruairi was Johnny's faithful dog. A very large, and very fluffy, black and brown dog who had been Johnny's best friend since the day he was born over ten years ago.

"Ok, I'm sorry, you're right, I'm not! Come here," Johnny said playfully grabbing his best pal in a headlock-style hug, both of their favourite kinds.

"Right, enough of this, let's get going, you know what today is, so let's make the most of it," Johnny said as he ushered his four-legged pal backwards down the hole so he could follow through on all fours.

Johnny was wearing his stripy yellow and red t-shirt, faded blue jeans and red Converse shoes. His clothes were well-worn and grubby; just the way he liked them. His black hair was wild and unbrushed; it was always wild and unbrushed! He didn't see the point in using hair gel and disliked the barbers, *a waste of time*, he said.

Johnny had crawled through the rabbit hole tunnel countless times but his body still filled with excitement. The older he got, the tighter the tunnel got but the pitch-black tightness didn't scare him at all. It felt like a blanket around him, a magic one, bringing him into his magical world.

Suddenly, something grabbed his ankle. He froze!

He felt himself being pulled backwards and before he knew it, he was back in the daylight of the garden. He rolled over on his back to find his younger sister Lily-May glaring down at him with her hands firmly on her hips, and a look of annoyance in her eyes.

"You promised," she scowled at her big brother, her long blonde hair bouncing as she tossed her head in anger, "you promised you'd bring me with you to the party."

"Well, you shouldn't have told Mammy about my new coat being ripped," Johnny snarled back.

"I didn't," she snapped, banging her foot in protest, "I told you I didn't, *you* shouldn't have left it hanging on the kitchen chair for the whole world to see."

There was a silence between the two as they stared at each other.

She's right, Johnny thought, *she's always right*! But that didn't stop him being annoyed with her.

Lily-May was a clever girl who's quick thinking had saved her older brother plenty of times before on their adventures. She was tall for her age and loved to explore although she somehow never managed to get quite as dirty as her brother when she did! Her red Converse tapped the ground impatiently as she waited for her brother to answer her.

"Fine," he muttered after a few seconds, "follow me."

He turned back over and began crawling through the rabbit hole once again. He could hear his sister 'humph' with satisfaction as she stooped down and began following him through the narrow, dark tunnel.

Chapter 2

Master Willow Sings

"Ah, Miss Lily-May, I'm so glad you accompanied us today dear," Ruairi said as he greeted her with a loving hug on the other side of the tunnel.

Lily-May beamed as she tightly hugged him back. She was always fascinated when Ruairi and the other creatures talked to her once they crossed through to the other world beyond the tunnel. She knew Johnny was too, but he was just too cool to admit it anymore.

"Right come on you two, we've a lot of ground to cover to get to the well on the hill for the celebrations," Johnny said impatiently, "and don't you go slowing me down today," he snipped at his little sister.

"Slowing *you* down? Eh I'm the one who *always* gets you out of trouble… Big brother!" Lily-May snapped back.

She's right, again, Johnny thought, *she's always right*!

The trio began running through the deep, wild forest. They were all so familiar with the path, they knew where to place their feet without looking down. They slowed down as they approached the Golden River noticing one of their small friends waiting for them at the old willow tree.

"Hi Mae," Lily-May said as she came to a stop with a quick inhale to catch her breath.

"Good morning you pair," chirped the beautiful little robin Mae, "I was hoping you'd both come today. I can't wait, it's one of my favourite celebrations of the year," she sang as she flew down and landed on Johnny's shoulder.

"I know, me too," he agreed, "I said I'd have to bring Lily-May along for the first time this year cause I'm such a good big brother!" Johnny said as he gave his sister a smug look.

"Hmmm, well either way, you're both here now thankfully, so let's get going," Mae chirped knowing right well that young Johnny was acting the maggot.

Mae flew up to the highest branch of the willow tree that grew on the banks of the golden river. A few moments later, the entire trunk of the tree turned around to face the children as a hearty, deep voice bellowed "Good morning children, be my guest and hop aboard."

With this, a huge sturdy branch moved like a ribbon through the wind and gently landed down at their feet.

Both Johnny and Lily-May grinned as they climbed up onto the branch of Master Willow and sat down with their legs stretched either side of it as if riding a horse. Ruairi hopped up too and sat down regally beside them.

The branch majestically glided through the air as the loud, warm voice of the willow tree, who liked to be called Master Willow, heartedly sang:

"Oh hop onboard the tree,

the tree that can be free.

The tree that moves like the wind.

Oh the tree that is me!"

The children laughed at his happy song as they looked down below at the gushing, crystal clear water of the Golden River.

Ruairi and Mae were busy talking amongst themselves when the branch gently landed down on the other side.

"Thank you for the report Mae," Ruairi finished as he stood up to walk from the branch, "please fly ahead and bring my message to them. Tell Pádraig Buzzard and Joseph Stag to accompany you."

"What report?" Johnny questioned Ruairi as he walked down beside them.

"None that concerns you boy," Ruairi answered with a wink and began to trot forward.

Johnny still found it a little unusual that Ruairi was the king in this world. The moment Ruairi came through the tunnel he resumed the role of Johnny and Lily-May's faithful dog; slobbering kisses, waggy tail, poop presents on the lawn… But not here. He spoke eloquently, he moved with purpose and power. He still looked out for Johnny and Lily-May but in a different kind of way, almost like they were his children, the prince and princess of the magical wild.

The trio began running at pace again through the deep green forest.

"Have we much further to go to the well?" Lily-May asked through pants after a while.

"Not long now child," a voice answered from above. She looked up to see Angela Harris Hawk soaring overhead.

"I didn't notice you Angela," she squeaked back with a smile as she noticed a beautiful hill covered in yellow gorse bush.

A few minutes later they all arrived at the bottom of the hill. Everyone stopped for a few moments to catch their breath under the clear blue sky and warm summer sun.

At that moment, Mae Robin, Pádraig Buzzard and Joseph Stag arrived to greet them all.

"Message delivered Ruairi," Pádraig Buzzard said matter-of-factly, "although I'd question whether they will heed it."

Ruairi nodded and called Johnny and Lily-May to him.

"You know this summer solstice celebration is our most joyful time of year in the wild," he began as the children listened intently, "but this year we must be alert. The faery folk are a little too excited to hear that a human girl will be attending the celebrations this year for the first time in one hundred years."

"What! Why would that bother them? Haven't I been here before?" Johnny said with his nose a little out of joint.

"The faery folk are interested in your sister Johnny. They want to make her their queen, but this comes at a high price. A price too high for us to pay," Ruairi answered solemnly.

"A QUEEN!" Lily-May screamed excitedly, "Eh, WOW!"

"Eh, *not* wow child," Mae Robin chirped in, but just as she did, a great roar erupted from the top of the hill; the celebrations had begun.

"I'll explain all later," Ruairi spoke, "but promise me to be on guard you two. Do not talk to strangers and keep close. I have sent a warning to the faeries and I've got my best guards on alert. Enjoy the celebrations but don't forget what I have just said."

"Yeah, yeah, yeah," Johnny answered absent-mindedly as he sprinted off up the hill towards the celebrations, Lily-May following at his heels.

Chapter 3

Slippery Strangers

Lily-May had never seen such a celebration in her life. Everyone from the newts to the dragonflies, from the pygmies to the deer, from the wrens to the golden eagles, were dancing and parading around Saint John's Well, singing and laughing and having the time of their lives.

The well was simply a small pool of water on two large limestone rocks which trickled off down the hillside and eventually led to the Golden River. Lily-May had expected a proper wishing well like the ones you see in fairy-tale books, but Ruairi explained that this well was an ancient one. A natural spring for fresh water that had been there thousands of years.

Everyone ensured that Johnny and Lily-May were well fed with berries, dandelions and even nettle soup that the hare family had prepared earlier for them.

"Storytelling is coming up soon," Johnny said to his sister. He was still annoyed with her and was especially not liking all of the attention she was getting. Nobody fussed around him the way they did around her and he didn't like it one bit. But he also didn't like feeling that way towards her and went to find his good pal Finn Hare. He would cheer him up and take his mind off it.

Lily-May was sitting on the luscious green grass eating blackcurrants and enjoying the festivities when a voice interrupted her thoughts.

"I heard you're looking forward to the storytelling," it said in a low, smooth voice like chocolate.

"Oh yes absolutely," Lily-May answered as she looked around for the voice, "I love stories and Johnny said it's definitely the best part of the celebrations."

"Your clever brother is right," the voice answered just as a small brown snake slithered up on a rock beside Lily-May, "it's my favourite part too."

Lily-May had never seen a snake in the wild before, only in the zoo where she held one about twenty times bigger than this one, so she wasn't afraid.

"My other favourite part is when we all get to drink the water from the well, did your brother tell you about that?" the snake asked.

"No, he never mentioned that," she answered as Pádraig Buzzard and Mae Robin gave her a wave from a few metres away. She waved back and smiled while she continued to eat her berries.

"I'm not surprised," the snake said, "I don't think he's too happy that you're here with him this year. I get the feeling he wants to keep the best part to himself and not let you taste the sweetest liquid that will ever touch your lips."

Lily-May didn't answer, she just looked at the snake and began thinking that Johnny probably *would* do that today, he was in an awful humour with her.

"I've got a big brother too you know," continued the snake, "families are complicated, that's for sure. But here, I got you a cup of it earlier, I had an idea this might happen."

Lily-May looked down beside the snake and noticed a little wooden cup made from a hollow piece of oak wood that had some glittering water in it. She hadn't noticed it before but then again, she hadn't looked beyond the rock as she was so busy looking at the celebrations.

"Do we have to wait for a certain part of the celebrations to drink it?" she asked the snake.

"Oh no, not at all, I had some earlier with my mother and father. Mae Robin and Pádraig Buzzard had theirs as well when we got ours. Drink it now girl, I promise you, it's like nothing you'll ever taste again."

"Well ok then," she answered with a grin as she picked up the wooden cup and downed the contents in one gulp.

Chapter 4

Remember

"SHE WAS THERE JUST A MOMENT AGO," Mae Robin screeched in a panic, "just there, smiling, singing and eating her berries, I swear it Ruairi. I just blinked and she was gone."

The panic and fear that filled the air was like a thick smoke that got into every creature on the hill.

The birds were soaring the sky desperately searching below.

The bigger mammals raced wildly down the hill and into the surrounding areas frantically searching.

The smaller mammals and insects clambered wildly in blind panic searching the tunnels and thicket trails.

Johnny stood petrified beside Ruairi, frozen in fear. His little sister vanished, gone without a trace.

"I should have known better than to allow her to come," Ruairi quietly spoke, his head low with worry.

"There must be something you can do Ruairi. Something we all can do," Johnny cried frantically, "She saves me every time with her quick thinking and clever plans, come on, there *has* to be something… Think for Pete's sake!"

"Ruairi, what was that old story your grandfather used to tell, the one about those wicked foul faeries and the well," Mae Robin said, her voice full of fear, "Something about the entrance… I can vaguely remember my nanna telling me when I was a fledgling."

"You're right Mae," Ruairi perked up, "you're right. Let me think…"

Ruairi went quiet for a few moments and then quietly and slowly began to hum:

"Every one-hundred years on the Solstice day,

The foul faeries appear, though not to play.

A Queen they will seek to drain underground,

To save our magic world, a foxglove must be found."

"That's it Mae, the magical foxglove flower holds the power to open the door to their world and protect whoever holds it," Ruairi shouted.

"BRING ME FOXGLOVE NOW!" he bellowed across the hill.

Joseph Stag galloped to the bank of the Golden River where hundreds of foxgloves grew, their majestic purple trumpets swaying to the silent song of the wind. He grabbed a bunch with his teeth and passed it to Patrick the golden eagle who flew faster than anyone else could.

He brought the slips of foxgloves to Ruairi and Johnny's feet. They both bent down and picked it up.

"For Lily-May," Ruairi said to Johnny as he looked him straight in the eye and beckoned Johnny to place his foot on the stone of the well with him.

"For Lily-May," he answered shaking with the fear of not knowing what would happen next.

Chapter 5

Foul Faeries

Lily-May opened her eyes to a terrifying sight. A tiny creature with wrinkles and warts, its face almost human. But it had a long, hooked nose like the beak of an owl. It had two eyes that looked like black wrinkled currants with no trace of emotion. It's mouth stretched across it's face from one long pointed ear to the other, filled with razor sharp, yellow, broken teeth. There was a few thick, jet black strands of greasy hair around its face and over its otherwise bald head. Folds of wrinkles and warts continued down over its head and onto its neck and shoulders.

It was hissing at her, loudly, tauntingly, menacingly. She felt the fear filling up her stomach like a ball of fire and spreading through her every limb quicker than she could think.

"There she is now, our queen, awake at last," a shrill menacing voice came from behind the terrifying face, "Bring our *queen* to her throne."

The creature in front of her grabbed her wrist harshly and dragged her to her feet. Lily-May banged her head hard off the low stone ceiling.

"Ow," she cried in pain.

"That, my queen, should be the least of your concerns today," hissed the creature as he dragged her even harder across the damp, candlelit room of stone.

Lily-May knew she was in a cave, one deep under the warm earth's surface. She knew she'd been tricked by the snake.

Why didn't I realise I was being set up, she thought. *Ruairi told me to be wary of strangers. Mammy and Daddy always tell me not to talk to strangers and especially not to accept anything from them. Oh what have I done? Where is Johnny? I feel so stupid.*

She felt so scared. She burst into tears as the wicked creature pushed her towards a rusty old cage with jagged metal bars that ripped her t-shirt.

She put her head in her hands as the creature slammed the rusty metal door behind her.

"All hail the Queen," he shouted tauntingly.

She slowly lifted her head and peeped through her fingers to see hundreds and hundreds of ugly creatures the same as the first, all gathered around her cage. Their mouths watering, edging closer and closer to her. Her terrifying fear grew as they began to chant.

"Our queen has made it back today.

One hundred years she's been away.

Today her precious soul we drain

And regain our magic power again."

Chapter 6

A Leap of Faith

Johnny and Ruairi opened their eyes to find themselves on stone steps that twisted down deep into the earth, beyond where the eye could see. Above them was the underside of the stones that made St. John's well. They were sealed tight. Johnny wondered how they had got through them but his thoughts were interrupted.

"We don't have long boy, you need to run like you've never ran before if we're to save your sister," Ruairi shouted as his powerful legs galloped down the stairs, "just don't drop those foxgloves no matter what happens."

Johnny ran behind Ruairi, skipping two to three steps at a time as they went deeper and deeper into the earth, his heart racing with fear. Nothing but black damp rock surrounded them.

Suddenly Ruairi came to a sudden stop. "Shh!" he whispered to Johnny.

They were about thirty steps from the bottom of the stairs when they could finally see a large opening. There was hundreds of creatures all walking together as if in a trance to the centre of the room. Johnny nearly screamed when he saw what they were all walking like zombies towards. It was his sister. She looked beyond terrified. He reached out his hand to touch Ruairi's head. He needed to calm down and just touching Ruairi had helped him do that since he was a little baby.

The chant bellowed through their ears just as they saw one creature open the cage to grab Lily-May:

"Our queen has made it back today.

One hundred years she's been away.

Today her precious soul we drain

And regain our magic power again."

"NOW!" Ruairi shouted as he leapt from the step and soared to the cage Lily-May was in, the foxglove tight between his teeth.

Johnny mustered every bit of energy he had and jumped too, willing his body to save his sister at all costs.

The evil faeries stopped chanting and turned to attack the pair until they noticed the foxglove.

At once, they all began to scream in pain and fell to the floor trembling with their hands over their ears. It was as if they heard a noise so awful it was driving them insane.

Ruairi pulled Lily-May from the cage as Johnny hugged her tightly and quickly handed her a foxglove snip.

"Let's get out of here," Ruairi said hurriedly as he beckoned the children towards the stairs. They stepped over the trembling bodies of the foul faeries on the floor and began to run towards the stairway. Lily-May leading the way followed by Ruairi and Johnny.

Suddenly for the second time that day, something grabbed Johnny's ankle just as he made it to the first step on the stairs. He screamed with fright as the bony claws of one of the creatures wrapped tighter around his right ankle. He fell forward landing hard on the stone step.

Without hesitation Lily-May kicked the hand of the creature as hard as she could. It yelped in pain releasing Johnny from its grip.

"Thanks sis," Johnny said sincerely to his sister as he grabbed her hand and began racing up the steps of the stone stairs.

They were almost at the top when Lily-May stopped in her tracks.

"Where are you going my friend?" hissed the snake who appeared on the step in front of her. It suddenly wasn't so little; it grew before Lily-May's eyes to be even bigger than the one she saw in the zoo. The enormous snake was almost ten metres long and one metre wide.

Lily-May froze in fear. The snake opened its enormous mouth where four glistening fangs edged towards her.

Chapter 7

Good Magic

"Not today Uar," Ruairi bellowed as he leaped from behind Lily-May and grabbed the snake's tail. With one mighty swoop, he swung the snake with his powerful jaws and launched it from the steps down into the damp, cold earth below, on top of the evil faery creatures.

"GET US OUT OF HERE!" screamed Johnny as he grabbed his sister's hand and dragged her to the top of the stairs bursting through the earth and back into the light of the warm summer sun.

Ruairi bounded out of the well after them and the trio fell to the ground panting in each other's arms.

The hares and the badgers immediately began filling in the hole weaving through magical hazel and hawthorn branches as they chanted a powerful incantation to seal it for good.

"Mother Earth please keep us safe,

Keep those wicked creatures in their place.

Protect us from their evil ways.

Let us live in peace all our days."

Lily-May began to cry uncontrollably as Johnny squeezed his little sister close to him.

"I'm so sorry Lily-May, I should have been protecting you and minding you today. Instead, I sulked and let you nearly be killed.

I'm such a fool. I'm so sorry. I love you," Johnny cried to his sister.

"I'm the fool Johnny," Lily-May wailed back, "Ruairi told me to watch out for strangers and I didn't. I thought Mae Robin and Pádraig Buzzard could see the snake, so I presumed it was ok to drink the water. I'm so silly. I've ruined the celebrations for everybody now. I love you too."

Ruairi sat between the two children forcing them both to calm down with his gentle manner.

"We've all learned something from today," he finally said, "and everybody here must remember this day for as long as we live. We need to tell stories of this day to our children and our children's children so that nobody will ever face those wicked foul faeries again. We must never forget. My grandfather's story saved young Lily-May today. Make sure your story survives should somebody need saving in the future," he said to all of the creatures in the wild.

"Why were they after me today Ruairi?" Lily-May asked after the crowds had gone away, "I thought all faeries were nice like the wood faeries we've met before?"

"No child, unfortunately not all faeries are nice. There are some who turned their backs on their race hundreds of years ago and began using their magic for evil, exploiting humans and animals wherever they could to benefit themselves. This eventually led to a war between the good and the bad faeries. All the wildlife, except the snakes, fought with the good faeries. By coming together in unity, they had the power to banish those foul faeries underground to keep future generations safe. The snakes went underground then also when they realised they had chosen the wrong side to fight with. Most of them died out over the years but Uar is different, she is filled with dark magic. The good faeries and their allies created a powerful spell to keep the foul down below but because the magic at solstice is so strong, every 100 years the veil is weakened, giving them the opportunity to break free. They need the spirit of a human to break the spell, not just any human, one that descends from an ancient bloodline…"

"Wait, *she*, I mean, *we*, descend from an ancient bloodline?" Johnny interrupted with a shout.

"Yes, you both do, and a very special one at that but I'll tell you more on it when your older," Ruairi replied before being cut off by Johnny again.

"What! Seriously, what's special about it?" he burst excitedly.

Ruairi chuckled at his excitement, "Surely you must have wondered why you both can speak with me and visit our world when nobody else can?"

"Emmm, not really!" both Johnny and Lily-May replied in unison a little sheepishly.

Ruairi laughed out loud at their innocence before settling between them both again, "well, as I said, I'll tell you more on that when you're older but for now all you need to know is that there was a reason young Lily-May was targeted. And, we're extremely lucky that we are all sitting here laughing together now."

He finished on a solemn tone as the children snuggled into his warm body.

Chapter 8

Together We Stand

"I'll go first and try soften her up," Ruairi said as he made his way back into the tunnel later that evening.

"Good luck with that," Johnny said grimacing at the trouble he knew he was about to get into as Ruairi disappeared. The sun was beginning to set in the fading blue sky casting glorious sprays of oranges and reds above them.

"Johnny thank you for saving me today," Lily-May said to her brother as she grabbed his hand before he got into the tunnel.

"Well, it's not like I didn't owe you one sis!" Johnny replied with a grin, "Besides, you did help me out in the end… Although I'm sure we never would have dreamed about saving each other from anything as bad as soul-sucking faeries!"

They both laughed hard at this.

"Well, we're going to both need saving from an even scarier creature now once we cross back through the tunnel," she grinned as she squeezed her big brothers hand, "so let's take this one together for a change yeah?"

"Deal," Johnny said as he crouched down into the rabbit hole tunnel knowing what awaited him on the far side.

…

…

…

"Jonathan Patrick Magory… What time do you call this for lunch?!"

The End

The Truth About The Fae

Hi reader, I hope you liked the story. I could have used this page to be all factual and serious (and boring) but I decided I'd just tell you my thoughts instead.

I believe in faEries… And faIries. And yes, there is a difference between the two. *Faeries* are nasty, evil and generally just up to no-good. *Fairies* on the other hand, while they might have a bit of devilment in them, for the most part they are good, kind and generally not that menacing.

I know a lot of adults don't believe in the fae, but as 'they' say (I always wonder who *they* are by the way) 'There's no smoke without fire'… The first mentions of magical folk date way back to books from the 13th century, and these books were not for children but factually written documents.

My personal belief is that these creatures are ancient beings that were here long before us humans became all-consuming and thinking we owned the place. I think that they have evolved to a point where they have such a high energy frequency 'we' (the all-consuming and thinking-we-own-the-place humans) can't see them in our day-to-day, busy lives.

I reckon that amongst ancient trees and areas that have a naturally higher energy frequency, like beside natural water sources, mountains, undisturbed valley's etc. you've a far better chance of feeling them and, dare I say it, seeing them. You've got to sit still though, I know, that's a tough one, but you've got to. You've also got to free your mind of all the thoughts in there and let your natural energy buzz to boiling point (you'll feel like you're floating).

Whether you see creatures or not, it'll be a worthwhile exercise. Do let me know what happens. Oh, and maybe do this near some foxgloves… Just in case! EJ

P.S - There's magic in the woods child, everyone knows it, but *you* need to remind them.

I'll tell you a story

About Johnny McGory,

Will I begin it?

That's all that's in it!

If you enjoyed this book, check out Lily-May's latest adventure 'Hare Today, Gone Tomorrow'

DOWNLOAD OUR APP 'JOHNNY MAGORY WORLD'

SCAN ME